CENTRALITY - KEY TO THE COSMOS

and other stories

S.N. MAHDIA

Table of Contents

ABOUT

S.N. MAHDIA

Believe it or not, the stories in this book were all written by a high school freshman! S.N. Mahdia is a 14-year old student at Malvern CI, a secondary school in the snow-plagued suburbs of the great Canadian city of Toronto. She lives with her family of four in a quaint bungalow and manages to survive the homework and assignments with a lot of Soundcloud and ice-cream.

She loves to read and write her own stories and has to scramble for a piece of paper whenever an awesome idea randomly pops up in her head. Her congenial, ambivert personality can be felt from a mile away, and her lack of balance and grace is very amusing to watch

. She zones out very often, visiting fantasy worlds in her head as the French lesson continues, and she has a PhD and a Bachelor's Degree in procrastination. Fluent in French, English, Bengali, Exaggeration and professional Sarcasm, she is often very loud and loquacious, and enjoys having a laugh with friends.

One thing that has bugged her since the beginning of time is that she succumbs *very* easily to boredom, which can be a disconcerting fact when doing history projects.

Centrality
Key to the Cosmos

Everything is either a part of a machine, or is a machine. This insinuates, an ugly, greasy, metal contraption that simply is there for one sole purpose. But in truth, machines are beautiful; their parts working harmoniously for a greater good. In fact, human societies are a sort of machine - everyone contributes to their flourishment. Some contribute by ruling over others or baking bread or building houses as they are assigned and as per this reason, this machine doesn't break down often. There is always a rusty part or two and they periodically appear, but are quickly removed from the system. An example of a rusty part in the societal machine would be the constant conflicts - the protests, rallies, strikes and if considered on a global scale, world wars.

One machine that no human has ever bothered to truly think about is the one keeping them on their feet. The one circulating air into their lungs and water into the oceans. The one that keeps time running forever and makes thoughts run through their puny mortal brains. This machine is what I take care of, along with the rest of us gear-nymphs. Gaiapaix, the complex contraption moving the cosmos. The base, the key, the *centrality* of which every realm in the thousand universes can prosper.

Gaiapaix is a realm where we work in keeping your mortal world stable. With sprawling workeries made of pure mooncrystal, gears that turn with the magic of our fairies, and tall skyscrapers made of shining lapis lazuli in which we sleep, it was a marvel to look at. This world was a beautiful, extraterrestrial (but in Earth's core) factory that kept your ungrateful mortal lives afloat for as long as you live (which, frankly, is not very long).

We were a colony in your core, the extra spine of the Earth, and we were charged with your healthy success. To be honest, the job was quite fun but required a lot of focus - if you accidentally leaned on a button you could wipe out an entire civilization with a *BOOM,* which has happened before. Pompeii was the result of my own old, old cousin Mateo Fayehorn of the Volcanic Activity Department, who fell asleep on the lever that detonated that active volcano. The Black Death started because of my great-great uncle Georgenry Fayehorn of the Health Department, who read the instructions wrong because of his lazy eye and entered the incorrect code, therefore causing an immense plague that wiped out half the population of Europe. And my great- great- great grandma Elyzania Fayehorn of the Cosmic Objects Department accidentally wiped out the dinosaurs by sending the wrong astronomical shipment to Earth.

Let me just say, the Fayehorn family is responsible for most epidemics and extinctions, and I'm one of them.

Now introducing me: Jaydiane Fayehorn, better known as Jay, current generation of the Fayehorn family. I am unfortunately known among my parts as the daughter of the family of destruction. Trust me, that title doesn't come with many perks. For one, I am never let out of sight, because who knows when I might accidentally ship the next astronomical shipment of bloodthirsty aliens to Earth (don't worry human, aliens exist. Most are flesh-eaters, so I wouldn't recommend attempting to ask them out.) My life was under a tight rein because of the stupid things that my ancestors have done and, if I was going to be fully honest with you, I *hated* it. I *hated* not being able to take a small nap in my chair at the Cosmic Colonies Management Department. I *hated* having someone escort me to the bathroom, and have come to believe they've bugged the toilet seats. I *hated* being watched all the time. It's like being on house arrest widespread across the entire country.

Today is no different. I am currently being watched by Butch the Security Guard, who is staring at a fourteen-year-old worker down a jug of Neptune's Finest Ale. That ale is why I still breathe today, and its deliciousness is something you mortals can't imagine. I forget the taste of the ale on my tongue and walk back to my cubicle, where I plop down in my cloud-stuffed chair and monitor the activities of the Goliath Drakons on Jupiter who are currently fighting tooth and nail over a blue lion steak. Yawning, I turn to my cubicle partner, good ol' Theodore.

"How's it going, Theo?" I ask, twirling a pen in my fingers.

"Well. It seems the Pygmy Gorgons of Pluto are currently sleeping. They are a bloody handful to take care of, and today of all days that responsibility falls on me," he groans. I smile in turn. His eyes are blue under the starlight lamps above us, and he sends a closed lipped smile in my direction. "How are the drakons?"

"Fighting over a blue lion steak. At least with those numbskulls you don't have to worry about overpopulation." I sigh, staring back at the screen, where three drakons lay motionless among the midst of the battle. One manages to get a grip on the steak and he runs off, followed by a mob of angry reptilian monsters. A shriek resonates through the screen as a different drakon now dashes off in the other direction with the steak, chased by the others. I turn back to Theo, who is watching the battle on my screen, mystified. "Snap out of it, Theo."

"Right, sorry. Anyways, care to join me for the party at the Ravenhorde's house tonight?"

"We've got a late shift, dummy. I'm not letting you bail out on me again." With my remark, he sighs in realization and disappointment and agrees to stay. Soon, we're back to monitoring the two biggest colonies of boneheads, managing their thoughts and their processes as per the manual.

It isn't long until it's near midnight. Theodore grabs another jug of ale from the mini fridge and we continue working on into the night before I hear a clattering noise off in the lobby.

"Theo?"

"Hmm?"

"Who's in the lobby?"

"We're the only ones here, Jay, and we are currently at a position of 1435 degrees latitude and 7025 degrees longitude facing east - therefore at our desks."

"I'm not kidding, Theo. I heard something in the lobby."

"Well, let's go check it out. It can't be more than a blind rat, but it's a great excuse for getting my bloody bottom off of this chair."

"Theo!" I protest, but he strides off in the direction of the lobby, his footsteps receding in the darkness. I groan and then leap up to join him. Staying alone in the dark was not going to happen. I catch up to his strides, and he stares down at me.

"Caught up rather quickly, don't you think?" He jokes, before ruffling my hair and making his way down the fairywood steps. I follow, staring around in the dark, ready for something to pop up out of the shadows. (No, I am *not* afraid of the dark. Why would you think that?)

The lobby is empty save for an urn laying on its side in the middle of the silverfish-patterned floor. I immediately duck behind Theo. That urn was the Elder nymph's prized possession, and was showcased in the shattered display a few feet off. Someone, or something, must have breached the alarm system and thrown it onto the floor.

"Blind rat, huh?" I answer the silence, directing it to Theo, who's gone as pale as a Uranian marmot. "Theo?" My voice quivers. With a shaking finger, he points out the eight glowing red eyes behind the display.

"Red-eyed drayko," he croaks before fainting in my arms. If you haven't figured it out already, Theo is Gaiapaix's biggest coward, which can be a very disconcerting fact when you have a run in with a highly lethal, acid-spitting reptilian alien.

The drayko emerges from the shadows and blocks the exit, its seven tails thumping against the ground, the sharp silvery spines on its back rattling against one another. Its two heads, with its huge, acid-drooling jaws armed with saber-like teeth, swayed hypnotically, trying to keep its next meal in place. All of a sudden the room was filled with poisonous fumes that smelled like someone folded Staten Island in on itself, releasing the world's nastiest smell. Its eight eyes fixed themselves on me, and I could hear it thinking: *yummy girl nymph with a side of a cowardly boy. Perfect dinner to bring home to my hideous wife.*

I bolt from the drayko, running as fast as I can go dragging an unconscious boy. His head periodically flops around and whacks the wall whenever I take a sharp turn, going deeper into the department. Soon, Theo's head has a nasty lump, but whether or not he has permanent brain damage is beyond the point right now. Being chased by a huge drayko is more of a save-your-skin vs whoops-I'll-be-more-careful-with-your-floppy-head sort of activity. Trust me, mortal, running for your life with a hundred and fifty pounds of scaredy-cat asleep on your back is not fun.

I pull the fire alarm as I race out the back exit, hollering at the top of my lungs.

"BREACH! THERE'S BEEN A BREACH! HELP ME!"

The lights in the houses around us turn on as the huge drayko barrels through the exit, destroying part of the foundation. The ground thunders as the moonstone brick falls, officially making it a large-scale attack. The creature rears on its hind legs and roars into the night, before focusing back on me. I hand Theodore over to a man who's stupidly hurried over.

"Here, take him." I say, before turning to face the drayko, who currently has lost interest in me.

The drayko stares hungrily at the hundred other delicious nymphs at the windows. It screeches, before stomping off to scoop up three kids out of a window. I grab onto one of his tails as it walks, before gathering the courage to climb up his scaly back, distracting the ugly creature. The fairies that have finally decided to teleport here blast beams of magic at the reptile, but to no use. Its puke-green scales are indestructible, but serve as great grips as I scale up his back (ha, get it? No? Come on, that was a good pun.) I reach his spiny brow, and scream down at the fairies, "Aim for the mouth!" They start brewing up a blue fireball, flames flickering and weaving themselves into Gaiapaix's most lethal ball of flaming yarn.

And then, I do one of the most dangerous things in my life. I poke the drayko in its unprotected, sensitive eyes.

It shrieks, opening its jaws wide as it roars into the poor ears of the once-asleep children. The nymphs take that opportunity and fling the fireball into its throat. I hop off the drayko immediately, hitting the ground with a jarring pain. A fairy rushes over to help, dragging me the same way I dragged Theo through the department, which, by the way, is painful. It immediately quits shrieking, its vocal chords torn apart before the fireball hits home - in its stomach.

Let's just say, an exploding drayko is absolutely disgusting.

It gets everywhere, scales shedding as its insides plaster themselves onto the nearby buildings. The smell of Staten Island seemingly increases tenfold, and the rest of it flops down to the ground like a deflated inflatable man. I shriek in disgust and horror as I realize what a mess had been made. Soon the authorities and the clean-up crew arrive and take me in. They question me, expecting to find that I made the mistake of shipping a red-eyed drayko to my department's doorstep, but instead I tell them it got in by itself which, of course, they refuse to believe. Why think that a lizard alien may have wandered into the department lobby on its own when you have a Fayehorn to blame?

Weeks fly by and soon I'm back in the renovated workplace. Theo is now up and functioning after I gave him a severe concussion. Security's been doubled, cameras tripled and they've unofficially bugged the toilets. I'm constantly being watched once again. But this time, all the extra eyes bounce off my thicker skin.

I was the one who poked a drayko in the eye.

I basically saved Gaiapaix.

I saved the centrality that keeps *your* worlds afloat.

I am now unofficially putting myself in history books by writing this amazing story for you puny mortals to read and gush over. And if you want to know about how Theo's doing, let me just tell you, he's still a wimp.

"Are you bleeding?" I ask Alyce, spotting the violent crimson stain on the sleeve of her floral dress. Alyce looks at her arm and shrugs nonchalantly, as if she hadn't been sliced open,drenching herself with her own blood. What a psychopath.

"Maybe I am, maybe I'm not. I don't know." She replies, yanking off her jacket and throwing it over the couch. I jump in her way as she tries to head to the bathroom.

"You need to get to the hospital!" I say, grabbing her hand and finally getting her to stop.

"Relax, Amber! It's just a scratch. Plus, hospitals cost too much," she says. I ignore her and shove her onto the couch as she yelps with pain. "Ow! What was that for?" Alyce complains, but as she tries to get up I push her down again.

"Don't get up, or I'll lock you in the fridge." I threaten, a deadly tone in my voice. I pull my phone out of my pocket and call Xander Mills, a friend of ours in the male dormitory halfway across campus. He picks up on the third ring.

"Xander at your service," he answers.

"Hey, Xan? Do you know how to treat a laceration?" Xander is a Nursing Major, and the only reason we each knew the other existed was because the nursing department and the tech department were working together on a project that Xander and I were both involved in. I press the phone to my ear with my shoulder as I get the first aid kit and the scissors. I cut away the square of red-stained fabric of Alyce's sleeve just above the elbow, peeling it away to reveal a deep, jagged cut. I gag involuntarily. Blood has always made me queasy.

"*Laceration?* Yes, I do know how to treat one, but who hurt you?" His voice sounds frantic over the phone. "Is it deep? Where is it? Is it over the stomach? Heart? Are you okay? How much blood have you lost?"

"Actually, I'm fine. It's my roomie's arm." Alyce snatches my phone and puts it on speaker so she can hear.

"Alyce? Oh." Immediately, all worry in his voice disappeared, and he sounded quite bored.

"Rude!" Alyce huffs, feigning hurt, and Xander laughs.

"Good evening to you too, Alyce," Xander says snarkily before he directs his words to me. "How deep is the cut?"

Alyce grumbles. "Laceration sounded cooler."

I grin. "Not too deep. Ugh, just get over here, Xander, you know what happens if I see blood. It isn't curfew yet and Garrick the hall monitor likes you."

"On my way," he says, ending the call. I look at my roommate, who's stopped bleeding. She tries to get up again and this time, I sit on her stomach.

Immediately she loses breath and flops back down. "Gerroff me," comes her voice, muffled from the cushions. I shift slightly so I don't flatten any vital organs, but otherwise stay put. A few moments later, I hear voices down the hall and a knock at my door.

"It's open!" I call, not intending to give Alyce a chance to breathe. The door slowly opens and Xander steps into the room, his blond hair messy and wet from the pouring rain outside. His blue eyes sweep over the scene, a box in his hands.

"Come on Amber, get off of her." Xander addresses me.

"Fine, fine." I get up, and make room so Xander can work on her arm. I look away, hearing Alyce's hiss of pain and head into the kitchenette to grab something to snack on. He finishes patching her up and looks over to me.

"Alyce, were you stabbed?" Xander asks. I stand behind him, trying my hardest to look as serious as possible while eating pizza-flavored potato chips.

"No."

"Then what?"

"Someone hit me," she says, wiggling her toes in the air. Xander ignores her actions and presses her further.

"With what?"

"A bread knife."

"Alyce, that's the *definition* of stabbing. Who did it?"

"Some guy in a ski mask. I went to my older sister's house to feed her cat Georgie because she's at a business convention in Ohio. I walk in and I see the broken window and two guys in dark clothing. I tried to grab the cat and get outta there as fast as possible, but they heard me. They shoved me against a wall and asked me who I was and what I did and why I was there. I told them the answers honestly, so they didn't catch me lying."

"What *exactly* did you say to them?" Xander looks over to me, noting my worried expression.

"I'm Alyce Wanderson, a student at Genesis University in downtown Fortegra. I am a computer science major in my second year. I'm here for my sister's cat Georgie." Alyce repeats what she said to the robbers, sounding like a parrot. I feel something cold race up my veins.

"Alyce," I say, my voice deathly quiet, "did you say anything else? Anything about project Osiris?"

"I only told them I was working on it," she says meekly.

"WHAT?!" Xander and I both erupt. Project Osiris was a project only tech and nursing majors had access to, but was well known across the world as a game changing team working on a game changing invention.

We were programming a new chip that could rewire a paralyzed person's brain and make them mobile again. The chip was already developed but had some glitches. Either way, the tech was weaponizable, greatly improving a person's nervous system and basically *upgrading* their abilities. For someone quadriplegic, for example, it'd give them back their legs. But for someone normal, it'd completely rewire the entire body system and make a superhuman.

"What is wrong with you Alyce?! That project is confidential! You can't go around telling robbers you work on a weaponizable project! It's like telling an assassin you have an unregistered sniper in your basement!" I yell, and she shrinks under both our gazes. Xander huffs angrily and the curfew bell rings in the distance, a low mellow sound in the background of my rage-filled ears.

"They're not gonna be able to break in here, if that's what you're worried about. We've got Garrick, and a lot of other security guards!" Alyce retorts, grabbing the bag of chips from my hand. Xander runs a hand through his hair exasperatedly.

Suddenly the alarm goes off in the hallway, and I hear Garrick shouting at people in the hall to get into their dorms and to get down low. Glass shatters in the distance, and I whack Alyce on the head as Xander slams the door shut, turning the lock. I hear a gunshot nearby.

"Look what you did!" I hiss at Alyce as heavy footsteps approach our dorm. "I bet Garrett's dead because of your stupidity! Next time I'll have to glue your mouth shut, you imbecile!"

"Well it's not my fault they were so demanding and intimidating!"

"It's your fault you *told them!*"

"Will you two just shut up?" Xander snaps at us under his breath, and we fall into a terrified silence as the footsteps stop in front of our dorm. I start muttering curses under my breath as I watch the doorknob twist ever so slowly. Xander motions for us to hide just as the lock begins shuddering and sluggishly turning. I grab Alyce and shove her into the closet with me and Xander dives behind the kitchen counter as the door slams open, light spilling out onto the dark dormitory floor.

Someone steps into the room, and for a moment, the sheer silence of the room slices through me, and I feel a tear trail down my cheek. I've never felt this much fear before. Of course, I felt afraid hundreds of other times, like the time when I let Alyce make us dinner, or the time I was taking a shower and I heard the smoke alarm go off because my grilled cheese sandwich had burnt to a crisp. This sort of fear- fear of getting your insides all over the floor - it's more terrifying than eating Alyce's *specialty,* artichoke soup (which, by the way, is revolting).

"Oh, Alyce," someone says in a singsong voice. I clamp Alyce's mouth shut just in case as the footsteps near the closet. They stop abruptly, and recede in the distance. Suddenly, a yelp echoes through the dorm and I hear a man scream in surprise and terror.

They found Xander. My mouth goes dry, my heart thudding against my ribcage. I look at Alyce, my hand still over her mouth, but instead of seeing her black eyes staring back at me, I see her lanky form unconscious over the cardboard boxes. She *fainted.*

How convenient.

I hear Xander whimper and yell in pain, and I ball my fists. I can't take it anymore.

I burst through the closet, an umbrella in my hand, breathing heavily. "Let him go!" I try to boom in a heroic voice, but my vocal chords desert me and make my speech sound squeaky. So much for the heroics.

The tall shadow that holds my friend by the scruff of his neck drops him, and Xander hits the ground painfully on his rear-end. He cradles his arm close to himself as he backs away from the man. I raise my umbrella, pointing at him threateningly. From where I got this sudden wave of bravery, I will never know.

The man turns to face me, his face hidden by shadow. His arm reaches out in the dark, and flips the light switch.

I blink against the brightness, my eyes not adjusting to the sudden change in light. When they do, I find myself face to face with a man that looks like a cross between Colonel Sanders and Will Smith. *What a terrifying thought,* I think to myself, unable to stop myself from noting his every feature. The man looks down at me, both figuratively and literally, because he is a *giant.*

"You certainly aren't Alyce. Where is she?" he said, his voice grating against the air.

I gulp. "Who are you? What do you want?"

"Me? Why, I am Rex."

"Sounds like something I'd name my dog," I mutter under my breath.

"Yeah," Xander pipes up from his corner. "Dude, you literally have the same name as my little brother's stuffed dinosaur. He's small, and green and cuddly. You sir, are not cuddly at all. Or green."

"I agree with Xan, your street name is absolute trash. You could've chosen something like *Bloodbath* or *Death Machine.* But you decided to go with Rex. Next time, name yourself Priscilla. Or maybe Princess Sparkle Nose," I huffed, and the anger on his face was visible until he went red and erupted.

"SILENCE!" he roared at us, and we obeyed. Rex continued his speech. "You two are insufferable!"

"Well, you're the one who barged in here anyways." I sass, hoping he won't put a bullet in me. *Might as well take a page out of Alyce's book.*

"Where is the chip?" he growls, irritated at us. Xander staggers as he gets up, planting his feet in the ground. I pick up the bag of chips from the floor and shake it in front of him.

"Here ya go. They're delicious," I say, and the man angrily swats the bag from my hand, and the chips scatter all over the floor.

"GIVE ME PROJECT OSIRIS! NOW!" He bellows and raises his gun. I duck. The bang of the gun rips through my ear and I grit my teeth in pain at the ringing. The wall behind me has a perfectly circular hole in it, the plaster cracked from the bullet's impact, and I look at Xander with a look that says, *run for it!*

Xander gets the message and bolts out the half open door. I race after him, hands over my head protectively to catch any other bullet Rex might fire at my skull. The man groans in annoyance and speed walks after us, alerting the rest of his crew. I grab Xander and we duck into a small corridor as Rex's men chase after us, a horrifying symphony of clattering boots, shouting men, and gunshots destroying glass and plaster walls.

"What should we do?" I hiss at him as we press ourselves flat against the wall as Rex's crew races past us. I breathe a short-lived sigh of relief before looking at Xander straight in the eye.

"Protect the project," he says matter-of-factly, not faltering over any word.

"Xander, this isn't some sci-fi movie where you're guaranteed to live and your sole mission is to keep the information safe! It's literally a matter of life and death!"

"Who said we have to protect the real project?" he says slyly, checking his watch. He looks up at me with the same mischievous glint in his eyes that Alyce has before she blows something up. Suddenly, I catch on to what he's getting at.

"The police are on their way. We just need to draw them away from the real prize without getting our brains splashed all over the floor in the process," I say. Xander nods enthusiastically.

"Okay, you got it. Amber Demarzo, I hereby order you to punch me in the face. We need them to think that we aren't a seamless duo, so if they think that you've punched me, then they'll think that we aren't that much of a threat to them. Plus, then we could get their attention and lead them to the other laboratory," he says.

"Okay, you've officially gone insane. I'm not punching you, no matter how tempting it is," I snap at him. To my horror, Xander pulls out a ballpoint pen. I've officially made matters worse.

"Stab me. Right here, where there's nothing vital" he says. He presses the pen in my hand and points to his thigh.

"Are you crazy?"

"Just do it!"

"I'm not stabbing you! That's way out of line!"

"Do it!"

"No way!"

"Amber, don't look at my face. Look away, and plunge the pen into my thigh."

"No!"

"I know you're scared and you don't want to hurt me and all -" He's cut off by me slapping him across the face.

"I'm going to kick you in the jackie if you don't shut up right now." I warn him, jabbing a finger threateningly into his chest.

"Okay, that works too," he says. I kick him between his legs hard enough so his cry of pain gets the attention of the criminals just stalking outside where we hid. It works, and he lets out a loud yell of pain, immediately drawing the attention of Rex's men towards us. His face goes red as he starts running lopsidedly, and I winced apologetically.

"They're over there!" someone shouts, and I drag Xander with me, heading towards STEM Lab 415 where the first-years were designing miniature motherboards.

"Protect the chips!" I purposely yell at Xander as they chase us into the lab. I grab a few motherboards off the tables and hug them to my chest protectively. Xander and I pretend to make a run for it, but Rex's crew barricades the exit.

"Got you now." One smiles at us triumphantly, and Rex pushes through his crew of men, coming face to face with us.

"You really thought you could *run* from Rex?" He steps closer to us. "Give me those chips."

"What do you even want from Project Osiris?" I say, my voice slightly trembling at the sight of at least a dozen guns pointed straight at me.

"What do *I* want from Project Osiris? I want everything that it can offer me! Every neurological upgrade!" he bellows, arms spread wide as he takes another step closer to us. He looks at us, and notes Xander's red face.

"You. Boy. What's wrong with you?" Rex says, pointing at his crossed legs. I think I kicked him too hard. Xander looks at me once, as if for permission to tell him outright, before stumbling towards Rex. The man steps back in shock.

"She kicked me in the business," he groans before he blacks out.

Great, just great. Now I've lost my human shield, I think to myself. *Did I really kick him that hard? Does it really hurt that bad? Well, he did sprint halfway across the building in that condition. I'm sorry Xan. I probably ruined your chances of fathering some biological children.*

"Dang, woman, you got that hard of a kick?" Rex mused, prodding at Xander's limp hand.

"I'm not afraid to kick you too!" I say, backing into the wall. He just chuckles, and snatches the motherboards from my hands. "Hey!"

"Finally! Ha!" he bellows, handing the motherboards to one of his crewmates. "Hook these up to me. Now!"

The henchmen sit him down in a chair and hook up the motherboard to a monitor. *They're seriously not tech-savvy. That's not how you do it,* I think, trying not to blurt out corrections to their methods. Two henchmen bind my hands and feet together, and I let them, pretending to be dejected. Then the henchmen hook up the motherboards to Rex, clipping the wires to his forehead. As they turn on the power, the monitor suddenly lights up with the videogame, *Zelda.*

As I said, they were miniature motherboard prototypes from the *first-years,* meaning that instead of gaining superhuman abilities, all poor Rex got was an electric shock from their horribly engineered projects. Sirens grew louder and louder outside, and soon the room was lit with red and blue flashing lights. The other crewmen dashed out the lab in order to save their freedom, but to no avail. Instead, the henchmen ran straight into the waiting arms of the SWAT team.

Xander was starting to stir as the FBI came barging into the lab, shouting at us to get our hands up. They noticed us in the back of the lab and three agents came over to untie me, while the other two carefully unhooked Rex from the motherboards.

As soon as they got the gag out of my mouth, I crawled over to Xander's side. "Xan, I am *so* sorry! I didn't mean to kick you that hard!"

"It's okay, Amber," he forces himself to sit up. "It worked, right? Project Osiris is safe?"

"Yeah" I smile at him, and the agent closest to me speaks up.

"Ma'am? You knocked him out?" she asks me. I turn to face her. "What happened here?" The agent gestures to the electrocuted and unconscious armed man in the chair and the monitor still lit up with the *Zelda* homepage.

"We led them into the computer engineering lab, and made him think that those motherboards were for Project Osiris to stall for time."

"And why did you kick your friend…?"

"Xander. Xander Mills."

"Yes," the agent continues. "Why did you kick him?"

"Don't worry ma'am. It was just for show. We needed to create some sort of diversion at the time to draw the bad guys away from the real prize, and I didn't know what else to do." I say.

"Wait," Xander says. "What about Alyce?"

The agent farthest away glances suspiciously at us. "Who's Alyce?"

"She's taking a lovely nap in the closet," I reply and quickly add, "she fainted."

"And was that just for show too?" the agent says, a small smirk tugging at the corner of her lips.

"No, Alyce is just a coward." I laugh, and stand up, brushing the dust off of me before helping Xander to his feet. We head outside the building and two paramedics come to give us a checkup. Policemen escort students outside, and I spot my roomie who immediately runs over to me for a hug. "I'm sorry Amber, this was all my fault! Are you okay? I did all this!" she wails.

"Yes, Alyce, this was your fault. Now, thanks to you, Xander and I are gonna be famous for saving Project Osiris," I say smugly.

"And what did I do? I can't seem to remember," she asks me, eager to hear her part in it all.

"You took a lovely catnap in the jacket closet. Slept through the whole thing, actually. Wonder how you did it, with all the ruckus." Disbelief paints her face and I brace myself for the impact of her next words, chuckling to myself.

"I DID WHAT?"

GREMLOCH'S ASYLUM
HORROR SHORT STORY

His hair flows around in the wind, coattails billowing. He walks forward, leaves racing through the gap between us. The gloom seems to press down from the sky and the fear spikes in my chest as he pulls out a revolver and fires.

Time slows down as the bullet rips through my flesh, jolting me awake. I gasp and immediately find myself looking for a hole in my arm, or maybe a waterfall of red blood. I find nothing but glistening sweat and rumpled bed sheets. I wrap my arms around myself. It was the seventh time this week I'd had the same nightmare. I'd wake up and ask myself if I knew the man with the revolver but I hadn't a clue who might have been.

I stumble out of a cramped cot. That was when I realized something was wrong. Extremely wrong.

My usual bed sheets were a light pink, prim, and trimmed with lace. These were dirty and grey, with holes from cigarette burns and rips and tears in the worn, smelly fabric. Not to mention the fact that I have a loft bed, not a cot. Where was my stuffed animals' corner? My computer table? My *window?*

That's when it finally sank in. I wasn't in my bedroom anymore.

The room I'm in smells like mold and damp cloth, a small steel table carelessly pushed into the corner. An old heart monitor sits beside it, wires ripped out, the screen covered in a film of grime, with cracks like spider webs across the front. I take a closer look at the steel table and see it lined with rusty medical instruments. *An old hospital* I tell myself, a sick feeling rising up in my stomach. I dash over to a corner of the room, intending to puke, but find myself unable to. *When was the last time I ate?*

Questions drown my brain. *Why am I here? Where is here? Was I kidnapped? Who kidnapped me? Why was I abducted?* They race after one another like greyhounds pursuing a steed, fast and furiously, unwilling to give the steed a two-second breather. I try to calm myself down, panting heavily and grasping the sides of my head as I count to ten and back seven times.

Okay, okay, calm down. First off, look for any impending dangers. Are there any killer clowns with chainsaws hiding in the shadows? I find myself analyzing every square inch of the hospital room over and over, before crossing that off my mental checklist. *Nope. All clear. Now look for an exit.*

I run my fingers along the wall, searching for a secret latch, or a button, or a certain brick to press like in Harry Potter and the wall between the pub and Diagon Alley. Suddenly, my fingers push against an irregular part of the wall and it slides away, opening onto a dark hallway.

Just like in the movies.

I walk along the hallway, hand trailing along the right wall to help with navigation, unsure of what else to do, a strange sense of terror settling in my stomach.

Something latches onto my shoulder from behind, and I scream, whipping around to face whatever it was. Color drains from my face as my voice deserts me completely.

A rotted corpse in a hospital gown grins at me with moldy teeth. I turn and run.

My footsteps aren't the only ones following me. I hear thousands of other footsteps, thundering like a stampede of bison from down the hall as I turn random corners and run for my life. A strange ache reverberates in my chest as I pass by a sign that says *Gremloch's Mental Asylum.* I gasp for breath as I realize what I'm dealing with: *insane zombies.*

The words etch themselves into my brain as I run straight for a pair of doors with a half-broken exit sign, praying to God that it really could be a way out of here, that all this was just another nightmare.

I ram through the doors only to find an operating room and a few men in doctor's scrubs. They turn to face me. Immediately, I regret being born with functioning eyes.

Their jaws are half rotten, gone, a gash in their heads revealing something pink, some covered in maggots, others covered with dried blood. Their eyes bulge out of their sockets and their flesh is a sickly color, dried blood staining half their faces. My stomach drops into my feet and my head spins as I turn around, intending to leave. Instead, I'm met with a wall of corpses, each grinning creepily at a poor girl surrounded by the undead.

The doctor closest to me seizes me, speaking into my ear.

"Oh, young one, why do you run away? Why not stay here, where you could have some fun?" His voice sounds like nails on a chalkboard, sending terror shooting up my spine. I scream and try to wriggle out of his grasp, fighting tooth and nail, before something heavy hits the back of my head and I collapse to the floor, darkness overtaking me.

I wake up once again in a bed, and relief rushes through me. *It was just a dream.* Immediately, I try to move my arms and legs, try to turn my head. I'm immobilized and all of a sudden, I feel like puking. No, it wasn't a dream. I'm still here.

The dead doctor hangs his mutilated head over me, smiling with his rotten jaws. I recoil at the stench, my mind screaming in terror as the doctor raises his hand above my head. In it is a scalpel, rusty and dull. My mouth moves, but it doesn't make a sound. Silence deafens my ears, stuffing them with cotton.

"Welcome to the Asylum, where everyone can be insane," he cackles, before bringing down the scalpel hard.

A sharp pain erupts through my head and the last thing I see is the smiling doctor, before my vision is hijacked by the blood running down my face. I want to wipe it away but I can't. I can barely breathe now.

Where everyone can be insane, the corpse's words repeat themselves in my head before I feel myself go more limp than before, staring emptilessly into the ceiling. A final thought runs through my mind, a repetition of the doctor's words playing in my mind like a tape on rewind.

Where everyone can be insane.

The Law o' the Seas
The Blunders of Three Stowaways

GHOST: Pirates are always seen as smelly, unshaven men on a giant boat made of wood waving around knives that they really, *really* shouldn't be waving around. People always think that pirates are rotten people that slash and steal, shove people overboard, pillage and burn. According to those people, pirates are large, overgrown men that have no care for anything other than gold and treasure.

Well, they're mostly right. They really are smelly, they don't like to shave, and they *love* to steal. But after accidentally 'waltzing' into a pirate crew along with my three companions, I can say there are more to pirates than killing and gold, and my two friends can back me up on this.

In all the movies, a pirate ship is shown as a ruthless monarchy where people would happily feed a comrade to the sharks in order to gain higher status. That, in fact, is a myth. Once you're accepted into a pirate's crew, you won't be thrown out. In fact, these crews have blood bonds, and if one person is dangerously close to the edge of the boat, they'll be quickly yanked back onto the safety of the deck and fawned over for a good half an hour before the work schedule continues. Nobody can break this blood bond. Heck, it isn't even made of blood. It's made of steel. Steel and PVA glue. Did you know that pirates use a gallon of PVA glue every week?

FARRAGON: Ghost, that sounds really, really dumb. You're ruining the voice note. Here, lemme narrate the beginning instead.

GHOST: No, I'm not ruining it, you are! Shut your trap, *Fartagon*! Anyway, I apologize for the interruption dear listener (or reader, if the voice note has been translated into text). Back to the story.

FARRAGON: (*in the distance*): Knucklehead!

GHOST: Ignore her. She's gone mad in the head.

Well, the only reason why solely me and my friends know about the true meaning of being a pirate is (as I hinted at before), we were stowaways on the ship of the most feared pirate in all the seven seas: Captain Kelpie.

The name wasn't very ferocious, but the meaning behind it was. Farragon, the annoying little brat that interrupted me just now, is from Ireland, where the kelpie legend originated. She tells me that a *kelpie* was a terrifying, shape-shifting, pony version of Medusa that lived in the sea. (Which drunkyard came up with this?)

But what gave Captain Kelpie his notorious status across the globe was all the pillaging he'd done! He'd sunken a great many ships, stolen boatloads of bounty, and occasionally fed his dog with the bones of his enemies.

Nah, I'm kidding. Captain Kelpie was given a false notorious cover. He was actually a captain of a crew of royally-approved privateers. They loved to steal, and pillage, but they had their ways and they had standards, and they'd never kill a person by their own hand. They'd just fatally injure them, or push them off the deck and let gravity do the rest.

Of course when Farragon, Julio and I first saw Captain Kelpie with our own eyes (after he discovered us in his cargo hold), we thought he was a typical pirate and was going to kill us, burn our bodies, and feed our ashes to the goldfish he kept on his desk.

FARRAGON: Okay, *my* turn. Sorry about that. Ghost just gets too graphic at times.

The only reason we had gone onto the pirate ship was because we were trying to escape the stupid democracy of England. Ghost, Julio, and I had all grown up in the same foster home in Cornworthy, a very small and localized village. Almost everyone there was either a veteran or an officer on temporary leave. So when King William decided to childishly pick a fight with those of the Barbary Coast (they probably left this out of history books due to the extreme foolishness of this dumb, young king), all orphaned, fostered, and street youth were to be deployed.

Why? Well, the Barbary Coast was the capital of fearsome Barbary pirates, slashers and cutthroats, and England didn't have too many people to fight them. Long story short, the three of us bolted from the village and hit the road leading out of the region.

It was like something out of a storybook, three foster siblings running away from an impending war.

In reality, it wasn't much of a pretty escape we'd taken. Julio kept crashing into trees, there were irritating wolves that attacked us and took all of our foraged food, and Ghost *never* watched where he was going, meaning we had to haul his heavy butt out of at least a *thousand* different sorts of ditches and holes.

By the time we'd reached the sea at Dartmouth Harbor we were exhausted, but still determined to get out of the country. Little did we know that we were being hunted by the king's huntsmen because we 'failed to prove our loyalty' or some other bologna they came up with. Our faces were all over posters, and the bounty on our heads was worth at least a thousand pounds. Luckily for us, Julio somehow knows half the population of the country, so he was the one who arranged a ride for us out of England on a fishing trawler.

JULIO: Introducing me, Julio Cantirez. This is where I come in. I knew a couple of people at the marina at Dartmouth. I'd managed to convince my ol' pal Joachim to let us onto his fishing boat. I'd talked to him about getting onto the trawler unseen, so we were scheduled to sneak into the cargo hold of the seventh docked boat at midnight.

When the clock struck eleven and the moon finally appeared from behind the clouds, Ghost, Farragon, and I tiptoed towards the docks from our hiding spot under the bridge, and started counting the silhouettes of the ships against the dark sky.

"We're gonna be free! Hooray! No more England for us!" Ghost had cheered, jumping about like a seven-year-old who really needed to use the loo.

"You're going to jinx it. Shut up and help me figure out which boat to get onto," I said, trying to figure out if the mottled dark shape to the left of the fifth ship was a boat of any sort.

I had actually figured out which was Joachim's trawler, and the door to the cargo hold opened beautifully for us.

If only Ghost *hadn't jinxed it.*

As soon as we stepped closer to Joachim's fishing trawler, a flashlight swung its blinding yellow ray onto us, making us freeze like deer in headlights. They were marina security guards, heading straight for us.

Stupid Ghost.

"HEY! STOP RIGHT THERE!" The two patrollers raced towards us, waving their batons in the air. We had two choices: get cornered in the cargo hold, or run for it. So Farragon did the smartest thing, and chose the latter. She bolted off the boardwalk and towards Hook Bay, Ghost and I on her heels. While we were running away, I smacked Ghost over the head with an irritated look on my face.

"Ow!" He complained through huffs and puffs. Farragon looked back, with an equal look of irritation.

"That's what you get, you dunce! What idiot hops about and cheers while trying to *sneak* into a cargo hold?" Farragon snapped at him, picking up her pace as the security guards gained on us.

"Look!" I shouted, pointing towards another bleary dark silhouette of a ship. "Go there!"

Farragon had swerved dangerously towards the rocks, racing towards the open door of the docked ship. Maybe, if we could evade the guards, we'd be safe in that ship. It did look like it was out of use. So, we all jumped into the open ship door after swerving around a huge boulder, making the guards lose sight of us for a few minutes.

We landed amongst crates and kegs, and Farragon clamped our mouths shut with her hands, shoving us towards the walls.

The guards peered into the ship, sweeping the flashlight over the contents, before they gasped. Had they seen us?

"Mortimer! It's Kelpie's ship! Get away!" One shrieked, quite like a girl. [*Muted*] Not that I'm saying girls have weird screams or are weak, because Farragon is certainly not, I'm sorry, ow, Farragon stop it! Ow, okay, okay I'm sorry!)

The two guards immediately slunk away from the ship, and before we could second-guess being in it, the door was slammed shut, leaving us trapped in darkness, the sounds of whirring pulleys hijacking our ears.

GHOST: Not all of that was entirely my fault. It seems that Julio forgot to tell you about the fact that he squealed like a pig once the flashlight fell on us, which completely gave us away. If he hadn't, then I would've been able to pass us off as a couple of extremely realistic, misplaced mannequins.

Anyway, once we were in the pitch darkness, we could only rely on our hearing and smell to really make out our surroundings. A low growling sound and a sudden lurch that made Farragon faceplant was the sign that someone managed to get this rustbucket moving, which was a feat unto itself. A yeasty smell coming from the kegs told us that they were filled with smuggled beer. The hundreds of crates, chests, and barrels only meant that we were trapped in a cargo hold; which was our initial goal, actually. If we looked at it in a positive light, which the others couldn't, we had caught a ride out of England. But, unfortunately for me, Farragon is *such* a pessimist.

Finally, we heard voices. Somebody lived on this derelict ship?

Unfortunately for us, those voices were coming closer and closer. Soon, someone slammed open a trapdoor, flooding the room with light - yes, it was already daytime. Before we knew it, we were being hauled out of the crates by the scruff of our necks, dangling from the meaty hands of a huge, buff, pirate.

"Who ye be? Trespassers? Spies? 'Cause I'm pretty sure me Cap'n *hates* havin' a spy aboard his mighty ship," he growled, before dragging us out the trapdoor and onto the deck, where the other crewmates were gathered. I squealed as they poked at me with their cutlasses, wondering why this pale boy was on their ship. I looked up from the grip of the pirate and saw we were pretty far out to sea with not a sight of land anywhere.

I thought this was going to be the end of our lives.

Heart pounding, I looked over to Farragon, who went a sickly shade of white, and I turned to see what she was looking at. Immediately, all colour drained from my face as well, as if I wasn't pale enough.

A huge man pushed his way through the sea of crewmates, his tangled brown beard full of silvery beads and braided locks. He was nearly as wide as two of me put side by side and under his blood red pirate suit we could see the ripple of muscles. His steel grey eyes glared at all three of us, and I immediately detected the smell of urine, though I was eighty-nine percent sure it wasn't me. I guess the pirate holding all three of us must've smelled it too, because he immediately dropped us and we hit the deck painfully.

He stared at all three of us before booming with his deafening voice, "who're ye?"

Julio, always the bravest, spoke up first. "I-I-I'm Julio Cantirez… Umm, I think that this is all just a *big* misunderstanding, um w-we a-aren't spies or a-any t-threat to you or your crew…"

"Ye boy." The huge man prodded at Julio with the huge toe of his oiled boots. "Yer lookin' like a churro."

The crew erupted into laughter, and I myself had to hold in a giggle. Julio really did look like a churro, with his brown skin and dirt sticking to his body just like the sugar-dusting on those delicious Spanish snacks.

"And who the rest o' ye be?"

Farragon spoke up next, her huge black eyes wide and flitting nervously amongst the crewmates "I'm Farragon. Farragon Forge. I'm only 14 years old, sir, I'm just a little girl."

The captain looked her over several times, analyzing her build, before turning to me. I gulped and spoke.

"I'm Phineas Mcleary." My voice went up at the end. Did you guys really think Ghost was the name on my birth certificate?

"Yer *Phin-as.* Phyn-i-as. Arr, forget it." He looked at my pale form, my white hair, and my blue-grey eyes. "Yer what the landlubbers call an *albino,* huh? We be callin' ya Ghost."

That was the origin story of my new name. It is frankly a lot better than Phineas, no offense to any other Phineases out there.

"We're keepin' 'em, right? We better be. They're a real cute bunch!" Someone piped up from behind the crowd, and the crew slightly dispersed to reveal a very young looking girl with the muscles of a 22-year-old male bodybuilder. Julio went paler than before at the sight of the pair of knives in her hands.

Seeing his frantic stare at the glinting daggers though, the girl expertly flipped them into their sheaths.

"The name's Monika." She helped us up, dusting Julio free of dirt. She then turned to the captain, eyebrows raised in silent begging. It probably was her huge, brown puppy-dog eyes that made the Captain resort to officially keeping us.

"Alright, but where ye three come from?" the captain asked us. Soon, we'd delved into the full story of why we were standing on the deck of a pirate ship.

FARRAGON: Well, that was how we got into a pirate crew in the first place. But then there was the day we realized that being a pirate was more than just chivalry, pillaging, and singing sea shanties by the bow of the ship.

It was a calm summer night, our second month aboard Captain Kelpie's ship. We were quickly the favorites of the captain and the crew, and nearly everyone brightened up whenever Ghost, Churro, and I stumbled into the room. (Yes, the pirates had resorted to calling him Churro).

We were just relaxing in our hammocks with Kipper and Johnny who were gunners; operators of the awesome cannons, when suddenly we heard the thud of boots hitting the deck.

Everyone was in their cabins except for Stonebeard, who was our coxswain, the 'driver' of the boat. Everyone knew Stonebeard always wore flip-flops and had an issue with alcohol. So, Ghost and I grabbed our swords and Julio went to alert the others.

We emerged stealthily onto the deck and immediately spotted the caravel that was pulled up to our ship and the two dozen barbarians who had climbed aboard. When the intruders saw us they did the only logical thing you'd expect from thieving barbarians: they charged with a cry of war.

Ghost was smart and he cut the rope the barbarians were using to slide onto our ship, then throwing up his cutlass to block the swing of a lance from a very hideous man. Suddenly, the rest of Captain Kelpie's crew burst through the trapdoors with a yell and it became a full-scale battle underneath the full moon.

Julio was quick on his feet, knocking the barbarians out with his mace, anticipating every possible move before powerfully swinging the spiked club at their arms and legs and occasionally their faces. Who knew he was so good at fighting?

I, however, was not so quick and got hit in the face with the heavy end of a club. Hard.

Everything started fading in and out of my vision and I felt something warm gush down the side of my head. My mouth was hurting horribly and I thought I swallowed something sharp and painful. Not good.

JULIO: Ghost yelled Farragon's name, and immediately I whipped around to see her stumbling about, struggling to remain conscious. Soon, both Ghost and I had forgotten the battle and bolted towards her while screaming her name.

Farragon seemed to have a good sized dent in her head that kept oozing crimson and we shoved past the midst of the battle, trying to get to her before it was too late. She was dangerously close to the edge of the ship, dropping to her knees from the bloodloss, the barbarian standing above her sharpening his sword to finish her off. Ghost went frantic, trying not to get impaled as we attempted to reach her in time while full-on screeching obscenities at the barbarian through the chaos.

"GET AWAY FROM HER!" he screeched, slashing a man's arm open with his cutlass as he shoved him out of the way. I stomped on another intruder's feet before swinging my mace at his side, making him collapse in agony. But I didn't care. Only one thought was racing through my mind.

I couldn't lose her. Neither one of us could. If she died, the staple in our lives that kept us all together would've been shattered. We were the three foster siblings. The three runaways. The three stowaways and kid-pirates. There was never one without the other two. I'd go insane in under a week if I only had Ghost to keep me afloat.

GHOST: (*in the distance*): Rude! I'm not *that* bad!

JULIO: Come on, Ghost! You just ruined the theatrics!

GHOST: It is my turn with the mike anyways, *Churro*.

As we raced towards Farragon through the carnage of battle, we knew that we couldn't make it in time. We wouldn't be able to save our exclusive, pessimist foster sister.

Julio had begun to cry as we continued shoving past crewmates and barbarians. We were going to lose our Farragon. We were right behind her. Only a few more feet…

The barbarian that was about to slay her had raised his sword in the air, the sharp edge of it glinting menacingly against the grey nighttime sky. We watched in horror as he swung it downwards in a sweeping arc.

"NO!"

Julio screamed, but instead of seeing Farragon's dead body fall off the side of the boat, we heard the clang of metal on metal.

Captain Kelpie had come to the rescue.

"Get yer hands away from me crew!" he bellowed as he kicked down the barbarian and essentially beat him up with the hilt of his cutlass. Julio and I took this window of opportunity and raced forward, grabbing Farragon's limp body from sliding off the deck and into the sea.

I did a pulse check and inspected her wound. It was a shallow but long cut that seemed to have stopped bleeding. Half of her face was tainted red, her auburn hair plastered to the edges of her scalp with blood.

"Wake up! Farragon, wake up!" I wailed, shaking her slightly. Julio tried to rouse her then tore his shirt to dab the wound. Suddenly another shriek filled our ears, this one from a frantic and terrified Monika.

"What happened?!" She came to us, fighting off the barbarians that tried to skewer Julio to the deck. Monika's eyes went wide with fear as she saw Farragon's unresponsive state. "Churro, move."

Monika shoved Julio away and grabbed Farragon's shoulder before tilting her head and opening her mouth. She gave her a few rescue breaths, even more frantic than the rest of us. "There's something lodged in her throat."

Monika suddenly slammed her hand down onto Farragon's chest with a wham and something small and white flew out of her mouth. Immediately, Farragon started coughing violently, finally awake and struggling to breathe.

"Farragon!" Julio cried. Before we could tackle Farragon with joy and relief, Monika hauled us up from the deck. "Take her to the infirmary. NOW."

Julio and I picked her up from the deck and raced inside, not before yelling a thank you to Monika. She just smiled and tilted her hat, before dashing into the midst of the now thinning chaos to finish off the foolish barbarians, her cutlass in the air.

FARRAGON: I wasn't exactly conscious for most of the battle but from what they told me, it was a pretty bad one. If Captain Kelpie hadn't taken down my assailant, I wouldn't be breathing right now. If

Monika hadn't rammed her hand into me, I'd probably be dead.

After the battle calmed down and the intruders were driven away, the crew pillaged their glorious caravel of treasure. Captain Kelpie called upon all of us to speak underneath the mast. I had a bandage wrapped around my head and walked with a wobble, others had suffered milder injuries.

"Yer all have been gathered 'ere to celebrate our victory. To keep clean the unspoken law o' pirates. Ne'er leave a friend behind, or they'll soon be yer foe. Arr me hearties! Tonight, we celebrate our Farragon, Churro, and good ol' Ghost, who alerted the rest o' us just in time to keep them barbarians' dirty hands off our treasure! To all the fails and wins o' the past, to all the fails and wins o' today, and to more victories in the future. Cheers!"

He toasted with a jug of beer, and the crew erupted into cheers. Julio tossed Ghost up in the air in delight, Monika smiled at the scene by my side, and we all celebrated like party animals until the tendrils of dawn peeked out over the horizon.

GHOST: So, you see, pirates are always associated with bad misconceptions. But it's what people don't know that interests them, and that's why the legacy of pirates lives on today in your landlubber lives.

It's a bloodbond that we pirates share with others of our team, a mutual understanding of each others' positions that *no* government would be able to replicate. The only reason why we're still alive to tell the tale was all because of the single, unspoken law o' the seas. As Captain Kelpie once said, "never leave a friend behind, or they'll soon be yer foe."

Trek through the Jungle

Usually, Dojo was a more honorable person. He'd admit to eating the entire supply of dried apricots three days before the effluvium season. He'd carry you high and dry on his shoulders as he trudged through the tar sands. He'd even stay awake all night just to ensure no blood-thirsty Sanguinary Mandrills came clawing through our camp looking for some delicious *human* hors d'oeuvres.

So it makes absolutely no sense that he killed Maestro. "I didn't mean to kill him, Katya!" shouts Dojo, arms flying all over the place as he tries to explain the dead Siamese cat lying at his feet. "He just sorta flopped down and stopped breathing!"

"After you put *tiger lily* nectar in his cowfish steak! You *know* lilies are toxic to cats, especially lilies that grow in the effluvium regions! The regions have that noxious fog all year long!" I spit back, angrily gathering the basketpacks full of pans, ropes, flintstone daggers, and preserved food. Now that there was a corpse in the vicinity, we'd have to evacuate the camp and set it up somewhere else in the Tumany Jungle, otherwise the dead body would draw in the Rockhoppers.

Rockhoppers were like mutated wolves with goat hooves the size of dinner plates replacing their paws. They scavenged for dead creatures and would gladly kill several live ones as extra food to take home to their hideous children.

"It's not my fault he ate it!" he complains, kicking the cat aside and coming over to help me. He slung three basketpacks over his shoulder, giving me the smallest to carry. I huff angrily at him, muttering obscenities and start pushing through the spiny shrubs, hopping over fallen logs and twists of blue rope-vines. Pulling out my journal, I leaf through the pages full of hand-written and hard-won information about the creatures, plant life, and survival techniques in the Tumany Jungle.

A chilly but thin fog hugs the ground, a wispy concoction of vapor and radioactive particles from the Ukrainian Nuclear Disaster in 2432 New Era. The nuclear explosion displaced thousands of people, killed several hundred more, and mutated the organisms that lived here. Dojo and I were two people from the city of Kiev that were seemingly immune to the radiation and didn't grow an extra limb; we were ten at the time.

After the disaster, I'd taken Dojo and a couple others to the Tumany Jungle near our city because the survivors in the town were going crazy; the jungle was our best shot at escaping. Once you got over the fact there were freakish mutated creatures, poisonous plant life, and a toxic fog season, the jungle was a *way* better place to be than being torn apart by insane people.

Of course, you must be a Westerner, living in the Americas. You probably think that the entire Ukrainian incident vacated the area nearby, and that nothing lives there and will ever live there for the next thousand years because of the intense gamma radiation. Well, *I* am living proof that you were fed lies by the Ukrainian government. The disaster *did* kill thousands of people and animals. But it also created hundreds of terrifying new species, thousands of mutated creatures, a ruined city full of psychopaths and a bizarre new microclimate with phenomenally strange weather.

The other immunes that escaped with Dojo and I nearly six years ago are either in another region of the Tumany Jungle, or they've been eaten alive. I know, I know, life standards here are pretty tough. You've got to be physically and morally strong to be able to wade through poisonous fog and under mutated trees and know that at any moment, you could be eaten by a clan of horrendously ugly beaked lizards.

Dojo's hand on my shoulder brings me back from my thinking. "Hey, Katya, I'm sorry, okay? I'll get us another kitty," he says, giving me his best puppy-dog eyes. I sigh in annoyance. I know very well Dojo killed Maestro on purpose, and I won't forgive him for a long while after this, because *who* in their right mind thinks that it's okay to poison the "family" cat?

I shrug his hand off as I stare at the old pages of my journal, looking out for any red flags like a whistle in the air that announces the arrival of windbox pigeons, or a flash of red in my peripheral vision that declares the presence of the Blinker-Fox. Nothing triggers my survival sense until a huge *boom* is heard.

"What was that?" I whisper, backing away from the direction of the sound. Dojo protectively stands in front of me. Huge resonating booms are either a mega-sized land-croc or an explosion of something that fell from the sky.

"Let's check it out," he says, sniffing the air. "It smells like gasoline. Definitely not a land-croc." Then he just takes off in the direction of the sound.

I curse under my breath and follow him. Staying alone out here is a horrible idea. I hurdle myself over rotted logs, vines, and huge grey slugs, shoving the tallgrass aside as I follow in Dojo's wake.

We break through the foliage and emerge onto a slab of land still aglow with flames and the smell of burned tires and something fleshy. Shards of metal, plastic, and weird fabric boxes are everywhere. In the center of it all is a small hover plane wedged between two tarutaru trees, half of it destroyed by the impact force.

"There might still be people in there!" I whisper-shout to Dojo. He grabs a lance from my basketpack and slowly makes his way through the rubble.

"Why would there be planes here? Tumany Jungle is a restricted airspace and- Oh my god!" Dojo leaps backwards in shock, covering his mouth, and I hurry over to his side.

Well, seeing a burnt human is a lovely way to lose your lunch. No wonder it smelled weird.

Suddenly, I hear a groan from the rubble. "Holy *sneazels,* there's a survivor here!" I call over Dojo, tracking the sound to a pile of metal and dense plastic. With his help, I push the debris aside, and we finally spot the survivor, or should I say, *survivors.*

There's a boy, looking to be around our age, with messy black hair and terror-filled blue eyes. He's shielding a little girl in his arms and he's got a nasty lump on his forehead, several deep cuts, bruises, and a shattered left arm. The girl looks dissimilar from the boy, with kinky brown hair, a cocoa complexion, and huge black eyes. Dojo stares in awe.

"Hey man, you need a hand?" Dojo stupidly asks, and the boy seems to snap to attention.

"Mr. Demesky? Uncle Jorge? Is that you?" he groans, his speech garbled. The little girl looks up, opening her eyes.

"AHHH!" she screams, and Dojo covers his ears. I shush her, trying to comfort her, but the girl swats my hand away. "Don't touch me, monster!"

"If you think I'm a monster, then you clearly haven't seen the things that prowl this place where you've crashed. Now, we're here to help, so quit squealing like a yellow-nosed dingo and get yourself out of that crack in the earth. Staying close to the ground for too long could kill you."

The girl hops out, terror written all over her face. She keeps a distance from us but stays relatively close to the boy still in the groove. I crouch down next to him. Compared to the other bodies around the debris, this boy was extremely lucky he wasn't killed by the impact force that tore apart the plane.

"Hey, I'm not Demesky or your uncle, but I'm here to help. Come on, lean on my hand and I'll help you outta there." I say to the boy, and he painfully frees himself with my help, and the girl immediately runs to his side. He holds his hand to his chest, and Dojo starts digging in through the basketpacks to grab some gauze for their injuries.

The boy looks me up and down several times, eyes wide. I open my mouth to speak, but he suddenly dashes away from us, the little girl at his heels as they run.

"HEY COME BACK! IT'S DANGEROUS!" I shout and give chase, Dojo quickly slinging the basketpack on his shoulder and running after me. The two survivors dash into the thicket where the Sanguinary Mandrills hunt. I feel my legs burn but I continue after them. The mandrills are cannibalistic, human-eating, oversized monkeys with chalky faces.

All of a sudden, a shrill whistle cuts through the typical jungle din and I spot a mandrill, ready to pounce on the boy. I grab my lance and throw it at the beast's thick, corded neck, and it hits home. Dojo grabs several spears and machetes from his array of weapons and launches the spears at the mandrills hanging from the trees above.

"RUN!" I shout at the boy and girl and this time, they obey, screaming and following my wake through the shrubbery and past the crash site, Dojo coming in close after us. We just needed to get underwater to escape the mandrills - they *hated* water. The nearest lagoon was a mile away, but we had to take our chances. The boy and girl sprint for their lives but I run faster, setting a violently rapid pace for us to make our getaway. From a few feet behind us, the bloodthirsty mandrills shriek and holler, a deathly choir of screeching primates.

They swing from tree to tree, gaining on us, and Dojo fires a homemade pepper spray grenade into the canopy as I lead the survivors to the small cliff hanging over the Pure Lagoon. My heart thuds in my ears as I step onto the edge of the cliff with the two behind me.

"Jump!" I shout at them, and they fearfully stare at the clear blue water three hundred feet below, and shake their heads. Why are Westerners such ignorant little boneheads? What's another three-hundred foot fall into water when you've already crash landed from the sky?

"No way!" yells the boy, the words tearing out of his throat. The small girl wraps her arms around his waist and starts crying as the mandrills come closer. Dojo fires another shell at the mandrills, but they start forming a tight line, advancing on us in their greater ranks. "Katya! Do something!" shouts Dojo, grabbing the last spear from his belt. "Go already!

The boy looks between the water and mandrills, the water calm and blue, the mandrills bearing their stained, sharp fangs; and he chooses the wiser choice. He wraps his arms around the girl and jumps, hurtling towards the lagoon. I grab Dojo's hand and we jump off the cliff, the mandrills shrieking angrily as we plunge into the cold water three hundred feet below.

For a few moments, the weight of the water bears down onto me, bubbles floating up around us, and I force myself to break the surface, gasping for air. The boy and girl are treading water nearby, and Dojo surfaces a few seconds later.

"You saved our lives," the boy says.

"We wouldn't have had to, if you didn't take off on us like that," I huff.

"Sorry about that. I thought you were like the cannibalistic Amazon tribe members or something. I watch too much Discovery channel," he says, dark hair matted to his face.

"What's Discovery channel?"

"It's a channel where they - you know what, never mind. I'm Edmond Abbey. This is my little sister. We come from London." He points out his sister, and analyzes each of us, spouting out some water.

"Okay, proper introductions happen on *land.* Come on, let's get to shore," Dojo says. We swim a few feet out and away from the cliff face and start wading to shore.

I wring out my wet braid, clothes sticking to my body as we haul the other two from the water.

Once we've all managed to settle back onto solid ground, Edmond starts up the introductions again.

"I'm Edmond Abbey, and she's Emily Anne Pedora. We're adopted siblings from the east side of London. We've lived in the UK all our lives, and the only reason why we're introducing ourselves to you is because our hover plane crashed here on its way to Sydney, Australia. There was apparently something wrong with the throttle. Our adoptive parents are on another hover plane to Sydney, and we'd gone onto our flight with our Uncle Jorge."

"I'm sorry for your loss?" Dojo asks, looking at the stoic faces of the two Brits.

"Don't be. We hated Uncle Jorge, right Emmy?" Edmond says, and Emily nods vigorously, rocking back and forth on her heels. Dojo looks down at me, before we introduce ourselves.

"Alright," I say. "I'm Katya, and the big guy standing behind me is Dmytro- call him Dojo. We're both Anglophonic Ukrainians. He's my friend, and we've lived in the Tumany Jungle for six years after the nuclear incident. It's either the jungle or the city- and the city is full of insane people."

"I have so many questions."

"Well, the Ukrainian government fed the outside world lies about the disaster," says Dojo. "There are actually new species in this jungle along with hundreds of mutated ones, and there's a toxic fog season once a year. Katya and I came here when we were ten. We've survived the conditions for nearly six years and we know this place like the back of our hand. Almost.”

“Why aren’t we bloody dead? Shouldn’t we die from the toxicity in the air or something? We’re not used to living in radioactive areas. Unless you count being near Uncle Jorge’s laundry bin. Boy, was that traumatizing,” Edmond adds with a shudder.

“Actually, the trees absorbed most of the radioactive particles in the air. That’s half the reason why they’re brown all year long. It’s also a reason why we don’t eat from fruit trees.” Dojo points out.

“So how do we get home? Or somewhere safe?” Emily’s soft voice comes from behind her adoptive brother, still rocking back and forth on her heels as she shakes water out of her huge hair.

I chuckle, and Dojo gives me a weird look. “Safety? I’ve never used that word in six years. This jungle is far from it. Anyway, if we are to get you home, the best we can do is get you to high ground and wait. The peak of the terrain here is Steep Hill. Though it is restricted airspace over the radiation site, we can hope for some rescue choppers to fly by,” I say, as I lead the group away from the lagoon to a small, blue-treed grove hidden behind some vines.

“Come Edmond and Emily, let’s make camp for tonight,” I say. “The sun is going down, and unless you want to be torn to shreds by creatures that look like buff penguins on steroids, I suggest we make a fire. You’ll have to stick with us to get out of here.”

Dojo sets down the basketpack and we settle in the thick, overlapping roots of the nearest tree.

*****

It's been a full week with the two British plane-crash survivors by our side. I let Edmond read through my journal and let Emily organize the food basketpacks for our trek to the slopes of Steep Hill. As we arrive at the base, Dojo stares up at the rocky slope that seems to be unpleasantly steep, and sighs.

"Alright, troops. Up we go," he says tiredly, grabbing a nearby stick and using it as a walking pole. Edmond sends me a small smile, giving Emily a boost. The little girl takes it in stride and starts clambering up the slope as if it was just a leisurely stroll, following Dojo's lead.

I wait for Edmond to start heading up so I can be at the back of the group, but he doesn't move. Edmond notices my strange glance at him, and looks at me with a nervous expression. I sigh, pulling out the radiophone we'd salvaged from the hover plane ruins a few days ago.

"What do you want to say?" I ask, pushing him gently towards the rocks. "Come on now. Rockhopper got your tongue?"

"Katya," he starts, following me as I impatiently start scaling the slope. I glance down at him, his face already as familiar as Dojo's, covered with a thin layer of dirt, stray leaves stuck in his hair. "Yeah?" I call down.

"I mean, I just wanted to say thank you. For saving two strangers a couple thousand times in this hellhole. For not eating us like the tribes in the Amazon. And for giving us the best chance at getting home."

"Aww, enough with the sentiments. The only reason why we're doing this is because we're so bored of having to save ourselves so often that we wanted something different." I wave off his gratitude, and he sends a lopsided grin at me.

"How would *you* like to come with us?" he says, breathing heavily as he plants his foot between two boulders.

His words nearly strike me speechless. Go with him, to England? I mean, I've definitely thought about ditching this place, but there was always nowhere to escape to.

My emotions start pouring in, and my mind goes slightly foggy with so many questions. I answer with a well-thought, brilliant response that'll force him to clarify.

"*Huh*?"

"Come to England with us! You could join our extended family, never have to live the survival-based life you live here again, actually be a part of civilization, and rejoin society!

"Okay, there are so many things wrong with that sentence, Eddy. Survival-based life? Really?" I say, as I ponder his proposal.

"Come on, Katya. You know what I mean! You won't have to wake up every day wondering if it's gonna be your last. You won't have to treat cuts with spikegreen berries, or, or, run away from those blood-drinking monkeys! You can finally let the world know about the Tumany Jungle, and Dojo can come too!" he counters, brushing his hair out of his face. He grabs the radiophone out of my hand, pressing a few buttons aimlessly. "It'll probably get a better signal at a higher altitude," I hear him murmur.

Silence ensues, but I'm quick to break it. "What if I don't belong in civilization? What if I was meant to be here? If I suddenly pop back into society, who's gonna be the one to study the jungle? Being in Tumany is a role that we've played since we were kids. What happens if we ditch it?"

"Katya, you deserve a break. I mean, if you tell the world about your findings here, they're gonna definitely come investigate. You could pay this place some visits and help out the other scientists - like being a tour guide! Just like in the Jurassic Park series!"

"Jer-asick Park? Scy-entist?" I sound out the strange words, and Edmond gives me a meek smile.

"I'll help you adjust, okay? It's the least I can do for you," he murmurs, and I flash him a grin.

"Are you two lovebirds done down there?" Dojo shouts from above, and immediately our faces go red. Edmond starts spluttering, and before I can murder Dojo for completely ruining the friendly moment, red flashes in my peripheral vision.

Oh no.

"BLINKER-FOX!" I yell, tackling Edmond to the ground as a lithe, furry blur torpedoes into the air where we were standing a few moments ago. Dojo picks up Emily and sprints up the hill as fast as he can, pursued by one of the horrible creatures.

"What the hell is that?" Edmond curses, coughing slightly with my weight on him. I look up and spot another flash of their bright red fur, and shout, "ROLL! ROLL!"

We roll out of the way of another set of sharp-toothed jaws, the rocky ground digging into our backs. Two blinker-foxes snarl at us, their bear trap-like jaws foaming slightly at the edges, their slim, yet muscle-corded bodies twitching at the smell of live prey. Their ears, with strange, blinking white dots, lie flat in a threatening manner as they coil up their bodies to pounce.

I yank Edmond to his feet and I grab a nearby stone. I throw it with a fierce velocity, straight into one fox's nose. It yelps, and the other one pounces forward, snarling even more as I grab another stone.

"RUN!" I yell to Edmond, but as I glance in his direction, he's already long gone.

Huh.

He's got the hang of it.

Edmond is higher up the slope with the radiophone in hand, yelling into it and running as fast as he can over the uneven terrain. I throw a stone into the other fox's eyes and while it balks, I take the split second of reprieve and sprint up the slope.

I stumble slightly and to regain my footing and give me an advantage against the creatures, I loosen up the smaller stones as I run off of them, sending them flying in the foxes' direction. They bark in rage as they start gaining on me. Just as one is about to pounce, something whistles through the air and strikes it in the chest, obliterating it in a burst of blood and fur.

I gasp as I look up, whirring sounds getting louder and louder. I see a flare fly into the sky, a flash of orange signaling our location. It had to be the work of Dojo and Emily. I try to get up, but stumble and fall.

Suddenly, a searing pain goes up my body and hijacks my vision. I scream as the blinker-fox closest to me clamps his jaws down onto my forearm. I try to shove it off while kicking at the creature, but it just clamps its teeth down harder, slashing at me with its sharp claws, drawing more blood than ever before. The whirring has gotten louder and louder, and I hear Edmond and Dojo shout my name.

With one last desperate attempt, I wrestle the fox off me before wobbling to my feet, then start running as fast as I can up the slope, blood dripping everywhere. A helicopter hovers close to the peak of Steep Hill, and I spot someone racing towards me. I collapse, numbness racing up my arm, fighting to keep my vision from being overtaken by the black stars floating at the edges of my eyes.

Dojo comes into view, slinging me over his shoulder before racing towards the helicopter. Once he dumps me onto the cold metal of the chopper floor, two masked people immediately start working on me: as they shove a pill into my mouth and wrap gauze around my arm. I stare at Edmond, who's holding Emmy close to his chest. The chopper takes off, lifting us to incredible heights.

"I guess we're taking a one-way trip to England," I mutter, as Dojo snaps a pair of earmuffs over my ears. The two nurses feed me a clear liquid, and suddenly, strength courses into my body once again.

"Not like we had much of a choice," he laughs, ruffling my hair.

Edmond pipes up, over the noise of the roaring wind. "If you don't have a fear of heights, Katya, then look down."

I obey, craning my neck to see the landscape below.

The Tumany Jungle stretches underneath us, a violent splatter of at least a hundred different hues. The sunlight overhead illuminates the net-leaf trees, creating an eerie yellow glow that cascades down onto the smaller canopy. Tendrils of blue-grey fog of the effluvium region seem to snake in and out of the tall gray-green grass, which sways hypnotically in the chilly breeze. The occasional screech of the mandrills echoes through the forest, a reminder of deadliness hidden under the canopy.

It's eerily beautiful, seeing the place I called home from a high perspective, seeing how easily the radioactive beauty can mask the terrors hidden inside.

ACKNOWLEDGEMENTS

First off, I have to say I wouldn't have been able to finish the book without the great help of Google. Thank you, Alphabet Inc. (and my FBI agent behind the laptop camera), for helping me find the research I needed, all while ignoring the absurd search queries I had made.

Secondly, none of this would've even been *possible* without the great Hannah Burkhardt (put your hands together and bow down low, the queen is coming through), who went from being my Grade 9 English teacher to being the *centrality* of this book. She was one of the first to think my stories deserved to be shared on a larger scale and thanks to her, this book exists. Without her, I'd probably still be lying on my bed fruitlessly writing stories. Thank you so much for sticking with me and suffering through all my pointless blathering (she did all that for *free! Can you imagine?!*).

Thank you to all the people that helped out; Renee Orchard, the next big Matisse, who helped make the amazing cover art (you're awesome!); to my pretty chill friends (you know who you are), who inspired some of the characters' mishaps, fails, and brainless chatter; to Allegra Swanson, who edited my story (and frankly made it so much better); and to my family, for supporting this throughout the *long* period of time it took for me to get my stories out there.

I must also thank Laura Smashnuk, my English teacher, who was the very first to realize I was (so-called) gifted at writing stories. You were the first to light a writing incentive in me, so wherever you are now, I hope I made you proud! Thank you Ms Smashnuk, for basically kick-starting my once-feeble story writing into something much bigger and better.

Thank you, dearest brain, for not bailing on me at the last moment. My brain and I had our arguments and then it'd hit me with that writer's block (deeming me useless for two weeks), but in the end, we managed to grind out some good ideas. (No thanks goes to the Procrastination Behemoth and the Instant Gratification Yeti in my head - always derailing my train of thought and making me watch countless animation and TED-ED videos on the history of cheese). All hands go up for my functional frontal lobe, that helped me come up with ideas for a bunch of stories, and I must give my childhood self a good ol' whack on the back for reading an unhealthy number of books, novellas, poems, magazines, and novels.

Finally, thanks to all the readers for reading this book right now and giving my anthology some actual purpose! Captain Kelpie, Theodore, Dojo, Amber, and Ghost Mcleary all send you bucketfuls of warm gratitude. On the other hand, Alyce, Jay Fayehorn, and Katya are all busy playing baseball with exploding hairspray cans (hmph, typical).

Sayonara, dear readers! Until we meet again!

"THE CRAZIEST IDEAS ALWAYS CHANGE THE WORLD. SO, IF I'M GOING TO DO SOMETHING GREAT, DON'T EXPECT ME TO BE SANE."
- S.N. MAHDIA

www.ingramcontent.com/pod-product-compliance
Lightning Source LLC
Chambersburg PA
CBHW020506160726
47991CB00007B/2830